MW00955929

I Don't Know How But I Know I Will

Written by
Krystal Cardona

Illustrated by
Mithini Wathsala

Thank you to all of those in my life who've inspired me to always believe in myself.

To my children,
May you always have the courage to be yourself,
follow your heart and dream the impossible.

To my husband who never doubts my crazy dreams,
I love you most!

I Don't Know How But I Know I Will

Text copyright © 2022 by Krystal Cardona

Illustrations copyright © 2022 by Mithini Wathsala

All rights reserved.

www.krystalcardona.com

Successful Thinking Mindset Publishing, Chico, CA

ISBN: 978-1-958471-00-5

First Edition

Ella got home from school and ran straight to her room.

"Mi Niña, what's the matter"
said mamá

"I'm not smart! All the kids
at school can read and I
don't know how" said Ella.

Mamá gave her daughter a big hug and said

"Mi niña, you can do anything you put your mind to, you just have to believe it in your heart."

Ella let out a big sigh as tears rolled down her cheek.

"But I will never be as smart as them" said Ella.

Mamá gently wiped away the tears and said
"Let me tell you a story about a little girl I once knew, Camila."

Camila grew up in a tiny village.
She was expected to follow in the footsteps
of her ancestors and be a farmer.

But Camila was different.

Camila was a dreamer.
She loved to speak her mind.

But above all she loved to follow her heart and
lived a world of "what-ifs" and big dreams.

One morning, Camila walked into class and there was a question written on the chalkboard.

What do you want to be when you grow up?

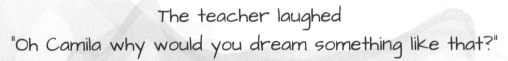

The teacher laughed
"Oh Camila why would you dream something like that?"

With a puzzled look on her face Camila asked
"but why maestra? I can do anything I put my
mind to, my abuelito said so!"

The teacher looked at Camila and asked a question she already knew the answer to "Camila, who in your family is a lawyer?"

Camila couldn't speak

The teacher continued...

"lawyers are really smart Camila and you struggle in school.

Besides, it takes a lot of money to go to school

and your family is a generation of field workers,

why would you even think this is possible?"

Camila stood proud
as tears rolled down her face,

"but when I struggle I grow.
I learn from my mistakes!
I work hard and I never give up!"

The maestra interrupted Camila and
shouted...

"Camila! You will not disrespect me!
It will be impossible for you to become
a lawyer! You will be nothing more than a
field worker just like your family."

Camila was crushed.
She grabbed her backpack and rushed out of class as the bell rang.

Ella looked up at mamá and asked "but why would someone say something so mean?"

Mamá smiled and hugged Ella tight.

"You see Ella, your imagination and dreams are just that, yours.

They are in your heart and a preview to your future and all that you can achieve.

No one else can see that but you."

"They are?!" Ella asked with a smile.

Si mi niña, they are, but only if you believe it to be true in your heart. There will be times that you feel frustrated and want to give up. You may say "I can't do this or this isn't working!" And when that happens mi niña,

I want you to remember the story of Camila, and remember what is in your heart.

And when you feel like you can't do something,
take a deep breath and add YET to the end of the sentence.

I can't do this...YET

This isn't working... YET

"Because everything you don't know is something that you can learn, and everything is hard before it gets easy!"

Ella looked up at mamá with a big grin and asked
"did Camila become a lawyer like you mommy?"

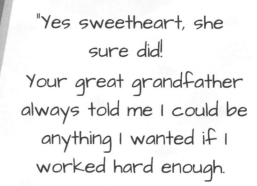

"Yes sweetheart, she sure did!
Your great grandfather always told me I could be anything I wanted if I worked hard enough.

So that is what I did.
I worked hard everyday and grew from my mistakes, but most importantly I believed in myself!
Just like I believe in you Ella."

Ella gave mamá a big hug and said
"Mommy, I don't want to give up on learning how to read, will you help me try again?"

"Absolutely mi niña, let's get started."

To learn more about Krystal Cardona's work igniting possibilities and connecting community visit:

www.krystalcardona.com

THE WORLD NEEDS
you
JUST THE WAY
you are!

Printed in the USA
CPSIA information can be obtained
at www.ICGtesting.com
LVHW060607071123
763219LV00001B/3